D0491313

Grandma Z

WALTHAM FOREST LIBRARIES

904 000 00642107

To Nanna F, Grandma L and Poh-Poh Y, thanks for all the food, love and stories.

And to Daniel B, who takes all of the above and turns it up to eleven.

In loving memory of Uncle A.

Grandma Z

By Daniel Gray-Barnett

S

SCRIBBLE

Waltham Forest Libraries

904 000 00642107	
Askews & Holts	23-Apr-2019
PIC	£6.99
6019730	

C

Published by Scribble, an imprint of Scribe Publications, 2018

18–20 Edward Street, Brunswick, Victoria 3056, Australia

2 John Street, Clerkenwell, London, WC1N 2ES, United Kingdom

Text and illustrations © Daniel Gray-Barnett 2018

All rights reserved.

Printed and bound in China by Leo Paper Products Ltd

9781925322156 (Australian hardback)

9781911344254 (UK hardback)

9781911344704 (UK paperback)

CiP records for this title are available from the National Library of Australia and the British Library

scribblekidsbooks.com

scribepublications.com.au

On an ordinary day,
in an even more ordinary town,
it was Albert's birthday.

Every year, no matter how much
he wished it were different . . .

. . . it was just like every other
extremely ordinary day.

'A robot piñata? Bake a cake?
Oh dear, no!' said his mother.

'You know how your father
feels about mess.

Now, why don't you put on
your birthday socks?'

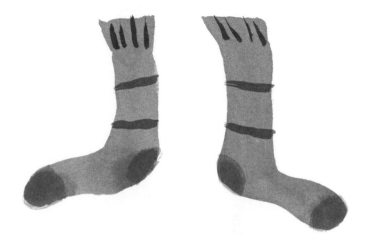

'Balloon poodles?
Musical chairs?
Oh dear, no!' said his father.

'You know how your
mother feels about noise.

Now, how about some
birthday toast?'

Albert closed his eyes and imagined himself
at a birthday party, holding a piece
of chocolate-cherry-ripple cake.

Then he made a wish.

Knock, knock, knock!
Albert's mother jumped.

Knock, knock, knock!
Albert's father jumped.

Knock, knock, KNOCK!
Albert opened the door.

Standing there was a strange woman.
But Albert knew who she was.
He had seen her in the old photo albums.

It was his grandmother.
It was Grandma Z.

'Happy birthday Albert,'
she said. 'Chocolate-cherry-ripple
is a marvellous choice. Shall we go?'

Albert got a fluttery feeling in his stomach
like one hundred Monarch butterflies coming out
of their cocoons. His skin began to tingle.

'Albert's not going anywhere!'
said Albert's parents.

But Albert didn't want to spend his birthday like every other day.
'Grandma Z,' said Albert. 'Where are we going?'

'Well,' said Grandma Z.

'You are most definitely going places!

But today, we're just off to do some ordinary birthday things.'

They went hunting for Dew of the Sea,
Thunder plants and Dead Man's Bells.

They climbed Enchanted Rock.

At the curiosity shop, Mr. McQuillen showed Albert the dragon's tooth horn.

They played in the Midnight Forest.

They went bird-watching,

where Albert spotted sandpipers on their way to Siberia.

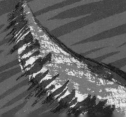

They built a palace with twenty-four bedrooms,
six fountains, a jungle-room,
a planetarium and a pastry chef.

The King and Queen of Osternovia thought it was so impressive,
they asked if they could stay for the summer.

They taught Icelandic horses how to can-can, rode the Big Dipper seven times in a row and discovered a new species of beetle.

'Albert,' said Grandma Z.

'There's one more thing this day
needs to be truly special.'

After the party was over,
Albert and Grandma Z went home.

'The next time my day starts
to feel ordinary,' said Grandma Z,
'I know who to visit.'

'My goodness!' cried his father.
'What on earth happened to you?' said his mother.

'I had a very unordinary day,' said Albert.

'And it was wonderful.'

From that day on,
whether it was his birthday
or any other day, for that matter,
Albert never felt ordinary again.

Not once.